Mrs Pepperpot Again

'Oh no, you can't fool me like you did the fox,' said the wolf.

'I'm not trying to fool you at all,' said Mrs Pepperpot; she had a good idea and was no longer afraid. 'You'd better do as I say or I'll send for One-eye Threadless!'

The wolf laughed. 'I've heard many old wives' tales but I've never heard that one before!'

'It's not an old wives' tale,' said Mrs Pepperpot indignantly, 'and I'm not just an old wife; I'm Mrs Pepperpot who can shrink and grow again all in a flash. One-eye Threadless is my servant.'

Alf Prøysen

Mrs PEPPERPOT AGAIN

Illustrated by Björn Berg

RED
FOX

A Red Fox Book

Published by Random House Children's Books
20 Vauxhall Bridge Road, London SW1V 2SA

A division of Random House UK Ltd
London Melbourne Sydney Auckland
Johannesburg and agencies throughout the world

First published in Great Britain by Hutchinson Children's
Books, 1960

Red Fox edition 1985

Printed and bound in Great Britain by
The Guernsey Press Co. Ltd, Guernsey, Channel Islands

Papers used by Random House UK Ltd are natural,
recyclable products made from wood grown in sustainable
forests. The manufacturing processes conform to the
environmental regulations of the country of origin.

RANDOM HOUSE UK Limited Reg. No. 954009

ISBN 0 09 931800 8

Contents

Mrs. Pepperpot and the bilberries

THINGS were not very lively at Mrs. Pepperpot's house. Mr. Pepperpot was in a bad mood—he had been in it for days—and Mrs. Pepperpot simply didn't know how to get him out of it. She put flowers on the table and cooked him his favourite dish, fried bacon with macaroni cheese. But it was all no use; Mr. Pepperpot just went on moping.

'I don't know what's the matter with him,' sighed Mrs. Pepperpot, 'perhaps he's pining for pancakes.' So she made him a big pile of pancakes.

When her husband came in for dinner his face lit up at the sight of them, but as soon as he'd sat down and picked up his knife and fork to start eating, his face fell again; he was as glum as before.

'Ah well!' he said, staring up at the ceiling, 'I suppose it's too much to expect.'

'I've had enough of this!' cried Mrs. Pepperpot. 'You tell me what's wrong, or I'll *shrink*, so I will!' (You remember that Mrs. Pepperpot had a habit of shrinking to the size of a pepperpot, though not usually, I'm afraid, when she *wanted* to, but at the most inconvenient moments.) 'You have something on your mind, that's quite clear,' she went on. 'But you don't think of me, do you? Watching your face getting longer every day is no joke, I can tell you. Now even pancakes can't cheer you up.'

'Pancakes are all right,' nodded Mr. Pepperpot, 'but there's something else missing.'

'What could that be?' asked his wife.

'Couldn't we sometimes have a bit of bilberry jam with the pancakes, instead of just eating them plain?' And Mr. Pepperpot gave a great sigh.

At last she understood; it *was* a very long time since she had given him bilberry jam, and that was what the poor man had been missing.

'Well, if that's all you want, I'll go and pick some bilberries this very minute,' said Mrs. Pepperpot, and she snatched a bucket from a hook on the wall and rushed out of the door.

She walked rather fast because she was cross with her husband, and as she walked she talked to herself: 'I've got the silliest husband alive,' she muttered. 'I was a fool to marry him. In fact, there's only one bigger fool than me, and that's him. *Oh*, how stupid he is!'

In no time at all she reached the spot in the forest where the bilberries grew. She put her bucket under a bush and started picking into the cup she had in her apron pocket. Every time the cup was full she emptied it into the bucket. Cup after cup went in, until the bucket needed only one more cup to be quite full. But then, just as she had picked the last bilberry into the cup, lo and behold! She shrank to the size of a pepperpot.

'Now we're in a jam, that's certain, and I don't mean bilberry jam!' said the little old woman, who now had a tiny voice like a mouse. 'Still, I expect I can manage to get the cup as far as the bucket if I push and pull hard enough. After that we'll have to think again.'

So she crooked her arm through the handle and dragged the cup along. It was very hard at first, but then she came to an ant-path made of slippery pine-needles; here it was much easier, because the cup could slide along it. And all the time little ants and big ants kept scuttling to and fro beside her. She tried to talk to them.

'How d'you do, ants,' she said. 'Hard at work, I see. Yes, there's always plenty to do and that's a fact.' But the ants were far too busy to answer.

'Couldn't you stop for a minute and talk to me?' she asked. But they just hurried on. 'Well, I shall have to talk to myself; then I won't be disturbing anybody.' And she sat down with her back leaning against the cup.

As she sat there, she suddenly felt something breathe down her neck; she turned round, and saw a fox standing there waving his tail in a friendly sort of way.

'Hullo, Mr. Fox. Are you out for a stroll?' said Mrs. Pepperpot. 'Lucky you don't know my hens are . . . Oh dear! I nearly let my tongue run away with me!'

'Where did you say your hens were, Mrs. Pepperpot?' asked the fox in his silkiest voice.

'That would be telling, wouldn't it?' said Mrs. Pepperpot. 'But, as you see, I'm rather busy just now; I've got to get this cup of bilberries hauled over to the bucket somehow, so I haven't time to talk to you.'

'I'll carry the cup for you,' said the fox, as polite as could be. 'Then you can talk while we walk.'

'Thanks very much,' said Mrs. Pepperpot. 'As I was saying, my hens are . . . There now! I nearly said it again!'

The fox smiled encouragingly: 'Just go on talking, it doesn't matter what you say to *me*.'

'I'm not usually one to gossip, but somehow it seems so easy to talk about my hens being . . . Goodness, why don't I keep my mouth shut? Anyway, there's the bucket. So, if you would be so kind and set the cup down beside it I'll tell you where my hens are.'

'That's right, you tell me. Your hens will be quite safe with me.'

'They certainly will!' laughed Mrs. Pepperpot, 'for they're all away! They were broody, so I lent them to the neighbours to hatch out their eggs.'

Then the fox saw he had been tricked, and he was so ashamed he slunk away into the forest and hid himself.

'Ha, ha, ha! That was a fine trick you played on the fox!' said a voice quite close to Mrs. Pepperpot. She looked up and there stood a wolf towering over her.

'Well, if it isn't Mr. Wolf!' said Mrs. Pepperpot, swallowing hard to keep up her courage. 'The ve . . very person I need. You can help me tip this cup of bilberries into the bucket.'

'Oh no, you can't fool me like you did the fox,' said the wolf.

'I'm not trying to fool you at all,' said Mrs. Pepperpot; she had had a good idea and was no longer afraid. 'You'd better do as I say or I'll send for One-eye Threadless!'

The wolf laughed. 'I've heard many old wives' tales but I've never heard that one before!'

'It's not an old wives' tale,' said Mrs. Pepperpot indignantly, 'and I'm not just an old wife; I'm Mrs. Pepperpot who can shrink and grow again all in a flash. One-eye Threadless is my servant.'

'Ha, ha! I'd like to see that servant of yours!' laughed the wolf.

'Very well; stick your nose into my apron pocket here and you'll meet him,' said Mrs. Pepperpot. So the wolf put his nose in her apron pocket and pricked it very severely on a needle she kept there.

'Ow, ow!' he shouted and started running towards the forest. But Mrs. Pepperpot called him back at once: 'Come here! You haven't done your job yet; empty that cup into that bucket, and don't you dare spill a single berry, or I'll send for One-eye Threadless to prick you again!'

The wolf didn't dare disobey her, but as soon as he had emptied the cup into the bucket he ran like the fox to the forest to hide.

Mrs. Pepperpot had a good laugh as she watched him go, but then she heard something rustle near the bucket. This time it was the big brown bear himself.

'Dear me! What an honour!' said Mrs. Pepperpot in a shaky voice, and she curtsied so low she nearly disappeared in the bushes. 'Has the fine weather tempted Your Majesty out for a walk?'

'Yes,' growled the big brown bear and went on sniffing at the bucket.

'How very fortunate for me! As Your Majesty can see, I've picked a whole bucket of berries, but it's not very safe for a little old woman like myself to walk in the forest alone. Could I ask Your Majesty to carry the bucket out to the road for me?'

'I don't know about that,' said the bear. 'I like bilberries myself.'

'Yes, of course, but you're not like the rest of them,

Your Majesty; you wouldn't rob a poor little old woman like me!'

'Bilberries; that's what I want!' said the bear, and put his head down to start eating.

In a flash Mrs. Pepperpot had jumped on his neck and started tickling him behind his ears.

'What are you doing?' asked the bear.

'I'm just tickling your ears for you,' answered Mrs. Pepperpot. 'Doesn't it feel good?'

'Good? It's almost better than eating the berries!' said the bear.

'Well, if Your Majesty would be so kind as to carry the bucket, I could be tickling Your Majesty's ears all the way,' said the artful Mrs. Pepperpot.

'Oh, very well then,' grumbled the bear.

When they reached the road the bear put the bucket down very carefully on a flat stone.

'Many, many thanks, Your Majesty,' said Mrs. Pepperpot as she made another deep curtsey.

'Thank *you*,' said the bear, and shuffled off into the forest.

When the bear had gone Mrs. Pepperpot became her usual size again, so she picked up her bucket and hurried homeward.

'It's really not very difficult to look after yourself, even when you're only the size of a pepperpot,' she told herself. 'As long as you know how to tackle the people you meet. Cunning people must be tricked, cowardly ones must be frightened, and the big, strong ones must have their ears tickled.'

As for bad-tempered husbands, the only thing to do with *them* is to give them bilberry jam with their pancakes.

Mrs. Pepperpot minds the baby

Now I'll tell you what happened the day Mrs. Pepperpot was asked to mind the baby.

It was early in the morning. Mrs. Pepperpot had sent her husband off to work. In the usual way wives do, she had made the coffee and the sandwiches for his lunch, and had stood by the window and waved till he was out of sight. Then, just like other wives, she had gone back to bed to have a little extra shut-eye, leaving all her housework for later.

She had been sleeping a couple of hours when there was a knock at the door. She looked at the clock. 'Good heavens!' she cried, 'have I slept so long?' She pulled her clothes on very quickly and ran to open the door.

In the porch stood a lady with a little boy on her arm.

'Forgive me for knocking,' said the lady.

'You're welcome,' said Mrs. Pepperpot.

'You see,' said the lady, 'I'm staying with my aunt near here with my little boy, and today we simply *have* to go shopping in the town. I can't take Roger and there's no one in the house to look after him.'

'Oh, that's all right!' said Mrs. Pepperpot. 'I'll look after your little boy.' (To herself she thought: 'However will I manage with all that work and me oversleeping like that. Ah well, I shall have to do both at the same time.') Then she said out loud: 'Roger, come to Mrs. Pepperpot? That's right!' And she took the baby from the lady.

'You don't need to give him a meal,' said the lady. 'I've brought some apples he can have when he starts sucking his fingers.'

'Very well,' said Mrs. Pepperpot, and put the apples in a dish on the sideboard.

The lady said goodbye and Mrs. Pepperpot set the baby down on the rug in the sitting-room. Then she went out into the kitchen to fetch her broom to start sweeping up. At that very moment she *shrank*!

'Oh dear! Oh dear! Whatever shall I do?' she wailed, for of course now she was much smaller than the baby. She gave up any idea of cleaning the house; when her husband came home she would have to tell him that she had had a headache.

'I must go and see what that little fellow is doing,' she thought, as she climbed over the doorstep into the sitting-room. Not a moment too soon! For Roger had crawled right across the floor and was just about to pull the tablecloth off the table together with a pot of jam, a loaf of bread, and a big jug of coffee.

Mrs. Pepperpot lost no time. She knew it was too far for her to get to the table, so she pushed over a large silver cup which was standing on the floor, waiting to be polished. Her husband had won it in a skiing competition years ago when he was young.

The cup made a fine booming noise as it fell; the baby turned round and started crawling towards it.

'That's right,' said Mrs. Pepperpot, 'you play with that; at least you can't break it.'

But Roger wasn't after the silver cup. Gurgling: 'Ha' dolly! Ha' dolly!' he made a bee-line for Mrs. Pepperpot, and before she could get away, he had grabbed her by the waist! He jogged her up and down and every time Mrs. Pepperpot kicked and wriggled to get free, he laughed. ' 'Ickle, 'ickle!' he shouted, for she was tickling his hand with her feet.

'Let go! Let go!' yelled Mrs. Pepperpot. But Roger was used to his father shouting 'Let's go!' when he threw him up in the air and caught him again. So Roger shouted 'Leggo! Leggo!' and threw the little old woman up in the air with all the strength of his short arms. Mrs. Pepperpot went up and up—nearly to the ceiling! Luckily she landed on the sofa, but she bounced several times before she could stop.

'Talk of flying through the air with the greatest of ease!' she gasped. 'If that had happened to me in my normal size I'd most likely have broken every bone in my body. Ah well, I'd better see what my little friend is up to now.'

She soon found out. Roger had got hold of a match-box and was trying to strike a match. Luckily he was using the wrong side of the box, but Mrs. Pepperpot had to think very quickly indeed.

'Youngsters like to copy everything you do, so I'll take this nut and throw it at him. Then he'll throw it at me—I hope.'

She had found the nut in the sofa and now she was in such a hurry to throw it she forgot to aim properly. But it was a lucky shot and it hit Roger just behind the ear, making him turn round. 'What else can I throw?' wondered Mrs. Pepperpot, but there was no need, because the baby had seen her; he dropped the match-box and started crawling towards the sofa.

'Ha' dolly! Ha' dolly!' he gurgled delightedly. And now they started a very funny game of hide-and-seek—at least it was fun for Roger, but not quite so amusing for poor little old Mrs. Pepperpot who had to hide behind the cushions to get away from him. In the end she managed to climb on to the sideboard where she kept a precious geranium in a pot.

'Aha, you can't catch me now!' she said, feeling much safer.

But at that moment the baby decided to go back to the match-box. 'No, no, no!' shouted Mrs. Pepperpot. Roger took no notice. So, when she saw he was trying to strike another match, she put her back against the flowerpot and gave it a push so that it fell to the floor with a crash.

Roger immediately left the match-box for this new and interesting mess of earth and bits of broken flowerpot. He buried both his hands in it and started putting it in his mouth, gurgling, 'Nice din-din!'

'No, no, no!' shouted Mrs. Pepperpot once more. 'Oh, whatever shall I do?' Her eye caught the apples left by Roger's mother. They were right beside her on the dish. One after the other she rolled them over the edge of the dish on to the floor. Roger watched them roll, then he decided to chase them, forgetting his lovely meal of earth and broken flowerpot. Soon the apples were all over the floor and the baby was crawling happily from one to the other.

There was a knock on the door.

'Come in,' said Mrs. Pepperpot.

Roger's mother opened the door and came in, and there was Mrs. Pepperpot as large as life, carrying a dustpan full of earth and broken bits in one hand and her broom in the other.

'Has he been naughty?' asked the lady.

'As good as gold,' said Mrs. Pepperpot. 'We've had a high old time together, haven't we, Roger?' And she handed him back to his mother.

'I'll have to take you home now, precious,' said the lady.

But the little fellow began to cry. 'Ha' dolly! Ha' dolly!' he sobbed.

'Have *dolly*?' said his mother. 'But you didn't bring a dolly—you don't even have one at home.' She turned to Mrs. Pepperpot. 'I don't know what he means.'

'Oh, children say so many things grown-ups don't understand,' said Mrs. Pepperpot, and waved goodbye to Roger and his mother.

Then she set about cleaning up her house.

Mrs. Pepperpot's penny watchman

STRANGE things had been happening in Mrs. Pepperpot's house. It all began when a little girl came to the door selling penny raffle tickets for a tablecloth. Mrs. Pepperpot hunted high and low until she found a penny; it was a nice shiny one, because someone had been polishing it. But just as she was writing her name on the ticket, the penny dropped on the floor and rolled into a crack by the trapdoor to the cellar.

'Bang goes my fortune,' said Mrs. Pepperpot, as she watched it disappear. 'Now I won't be able to buy a raffle ticket after all. But I can't let you go without giving you anything; what about a nice home-made short-cake?' And she stood on a stool to reach the cake-tin.

It was empty. Mrs. Pepperpot turned the tin almost inside out, but there was no sign of any short-cake.

'I can't understand it,' she said. 'I baked two whole rounds of short-cake on Friday. Today it's only Monday, and the tin is empty. Very mysterious. But I've got something you might like even better, little girl.' So

saying, Mrs. Pepperpot opened the trapdoor to the cellar
and went down the steps to fetch the big jar of bramble
jelly she had left over from the summer.

But what a sight met her eyes!

'Goodness Gracious and Glory Be!' she exclaimed,
for the big jar of bramble jelly was lying smashed under
the shelf with the jelly gently oozing out over the floor.
From the sticky mess a little trail of mouse footprints
ran across to the chimney.

There was nothing for it—Mrs. Pepperpot had to go
up to the little girl and tell her she couldn't even have
bramble jelly. But the little girl said it didn't matter a bit
and politely curtsied before going on to the next house.

Mrs. Pepperpot took a mouse-trap and went down the cellar steps again. She baited it with cheese and set it very carefully on the floor. When it was done she turned to go upstairs again, but the hem of her skirt brushed against it, and SNAP! went the trap, with a corner of her skirt caught in it. That was bad enough, but then, if you please, she shrank again!

'Now I really *am* stuck!' she told herself, and she certainly was; she couldn't move an inch. After she had sat there a while she saw a young mouse peeping over the edge of an empty flowerpot.

'You're quite safe to come out,' said Mrs. Pepperpot. 'I'm too well tethered to do you any harm at the moment.'

But the little mouse darted off to an empty cardboard box and then two little mice popped their noses over the edge.

'One and one makes two,' said Mrs. Pepperpot. 'I learned that at school, and I wouldn't be a bit surprised if you fetched a third one—for one and two make three!'

She was right. The two little mice darted off together and stayed away quite a long time while she sat and waited. Suddenly she heard a tinny little sound. Ping! Ping! And a big mouse came walking towards her on his hind legs, banging a shiny gong with a little steel pin. The shiny gong was Mrs. Pepperpot's lost penny!

The big mouse bowed low. 'Queen of the House, I greet you!' The little mice were peeping out from behind him.

'Thank goodness for that!' said Mrs. Pepperpot. 'For a moment I thought you might be coming to gobble me up—you're so much bigger than I am!'

'We're not in the habit of gobbling up queens,' said the large mouse. 'I just wanted to tell you, you have a thief in your house.'

Mrs. Pepperpot snorted. 'Thief indeed! Of course I have; you and all the other mice are the thieves in my house. Whose penny is it you're using for a gong, may I ask?'

'Oh, is that what it is? A penny?' said the big mouse. 'Well, it rolled through a crack in the floor, you see, so I thought I could use it to scare away the thief and to show I'm the watchman in this house. You really do need a watchman, Queen of the House, to keep an eye on things for you.'

'What nonsense!' said Mrs. Pepperpot. She tried to stand up, but it was rather difficult with her dress caught in the trap and she herself so tiny.

'Take it easy, Queen of the House,' said the big mouse. 'Let my son here tell you what he has seen.'

Timidly, one of the little mice came forward and told how he had climbed up the chimney one day and peeped through a hole into the kitchen. There he had seen a terrible monster who was eating up all the cake in the tin.

Then the other little mouse chirped in to tell how he had been playing hide-and-seek behind a jam-jar on the shelf when the monster had put out a huge hand and taken the jar away. But he had been so scared when he saw the little mouse that he had dropped the jar on the floor, and all the bramble jelly came pouring out.

Suddenly they heard Tramp! Tramp! Tramp! up above; the sound of huge boots walking about.

'That's the monster!' said one of the little mice.

'Yes, that's him all right!' said the other little mouse.

'Is it, indeed!' said Mrs. Pepperpot. 'If only I could get out of this trap, I should very much like to go and have a look at this monster.'

'We'll help you,' said all the mice, and they set to work to free Mrs. Pepperpot from the trap in the way only mice know how; they gnawed through her skirt, leaving a piece stuck in the spring.

'Now you must hurry up to the kitchen to see the monster,' they said.

'But how am I to get there?' asked Mrs. Pepperpot.

'Up through the chimney on our special rope; we'll pull you up.'

And that's what they did. They hoisted Mrs. Pepperpot higher and higher inside the chimney, until she could see a chink of light.

'That's the crack into the kitchen,' the big mouse told her from below.

She called down to him: 'Thank you Mr. Watchman, thank you for your help, and keep a sharp look-out!'

Then she climbed through the hole in the wall. As soon as she set foot on the floor she grew to her normal size. Standing in front of the stove, she put her hands on her hips and said, 'So it's you, husband, is it, who's been eating all my short-cake and stealing the bramble jelly in the cellar?'

Mr. Pepperpot looked dumbfounded: 'How did you know that?' he said.

'Because I have a watchman now, I have paid him a penny,' said Mrs. Pepperpot.

The bad luck story

IF YOU take the road past Mrs. Pepperpot's house and turn to the right, then to the left and carry straight on, you will come to a cottage.

In this cottage lived an old woman they called 'Mrs. Calamity', because she believed in omens and always expected the worst to happen. Another curious thing about her was that she had the habit of stealing cuttings from pot-plants in other people's houses. Not that this in itself was very serious, only sometimes the flowers died after she had been cutting them about. But Mrs. Calamity had the idea that stolen plants thrive much better than any you got as a present, which is just one of those old wives' tales.

One day she visited little old Mrs. Pepperpot. She sat on the edge of a chair very politely and talked about this and that, but all the time she was looking round at all the plants in Mrs. Pepperpot's window-sill.

'That's right; have a good look,' thought Mrs. Pepperpot to herself. 'I know what you're after; you want to take cuttings of my best geranium. But we'll see about that, my fine lady!'

Unfortunately, there was a knock at the door just at that moment, and Mrs. Pepperpot had to leave her visitor alone while she went to answer it.

A man stood there. 'Anyone called Cuthbertson live here?' he asked.

'Cuthbertson? There's never been anyone of that name in this house, as far as I know,' said Mrs. Pepperpot. 'You'd better ask at the post-office. Excuse me, I'm busy just now.' And she turned to shut the door.

Too late! For at that moment Mrs. Pepperpot shrank again!

She stretched her little neck as much as she could to look over the doorstep into the sitting-room. Sure enough! There was Mrs. Calamity ferreting about in Mrs. Pepperpot's flowerpots.

'I have a feeling you're going to regret that, Madam Thief,' thought Mrs. Pepperpot as she swung herself over the step into the yard. There she found a little wagtail pecking about, looking for something to eat.

'Hullo, little wagtail,' she said. 'If you'll help *me*, then I'll help *you*. You can have all the crumbs you want if you'll just go over to the front doorstep and stand quite still, facing the door.'

'That's easily done,' said the wagtail, and hopped across the yard.

No doubt Mrs. Calamity was wondering what had happened to the lady of the house. She came to the door and looked out, holding her hand carefully over her apron pocket where she had hidden the geranium cutting.

Then she caught sight of the wagtail on the step. 'Oh Calamity!' she wailed. 'I've looked a wagtail straight in the face and now I shall have bad luck for a year.'

And, clutching her apron pocket, she hurried away from the house.

But over her head the wagtail was following her, flying with Mrs. Pepperpot on its back. As she clung with her arms round the bird's neck, she said: 'D'you know where we could find a black cat?'

'A black cat?' answered the wagtail. 'I should think I do! The horrible creature was lying in wait for me down by the bend in the road. She's probably still there. So don't ask me to land anywhere near her.'

'Don't worry!' said Mrs. Pepperpot. 'I want you to put me down on the *opposite* side of the road—I have a little plan.'

So the wagtail did as she asked and flew out of harm's way as fast as it could go.

Mrs. Pepperpot crouched down in the long grass; she could see the cat's tail waving to and fro in the ditch

on the other side of the road. Soon she heard the clump, clump, clump of Mrs. Calamity's boots as she walked down the road.

Just as she came past where Mrs. Pepperpot was

hiding, Mrs. Pepperpot made the noise of a wagtail calling. The black cat heard it and, like a streak of lightning, shot across the road, right in front of Mrs. Calamity.

Mrs. Calamity stood stock-still with fright. 'A black cat!' she screamed. 'That means *three* years' bad luck!

Oh Calamity, what shall I do?' She was so alarmed she didn't dare go on; instead, she took the path through the wood to her house.

Meanwhile the cat was going in the same direction, for by now Mrs. Pepperpot was riding on her back. 'Have you seen any magpies about?' she asked the cat.

'I should think I have!' said the cat. 'There's a pair of them in that birch-tree over there; they tease me and pull my tail whenever they get the chance. Look! They're waiting for me now!'

'Then you can drop me here,' said Mrs. Pepperpot. 'Come and see me tomorrow and I'll give you a bowl of cream.'

The cat did as she asked, and a moment later Mrs. Pepperpot was talking to the magpies in the birch-tree.

'Good afternoon,' she said. 'I wonder if you would have such a thing as a key-ring in your nest?'

'Oh no,' said the magpies, 'we don't have key-rings, we only collect broken-mirror bits.'

'The best is good enough,' replied Mrs. Pepperpot. 'I want you to put some nice-looking bits on Mrs. Calamity's doorstep. If you can do that for me, I'll keep the curly tail for you when we kill the pig at Christmas.'

The magpies didn't need to be told twice. A little heap of broken-mirror bits were on Mrs. Calamity's doorstep before you could say Jack Robinson.

When she arrived and saw what was waiting for her Mrs. Calamity sat down and cried.

'Oh, misery me! Oh Calamity! A broken mirror will give me *seven* years' bad luck!'

But by now Mrs. Pepperpot had grown to her proper size again; quietly she came round the corner, and her voice was quite gentle when she spoke.

'Now, now, Mrs. Calamity,' she said, 'you mustn't sit here crying.'

'Oh, Mrs. Pepperpot! It's nothing but bad luck for me from beginning to end.' She sniffed, and she told Mrs. Pepperpot about the wagtail that had faced her, the cat that had jumped across her path and now the broken mirror. When she'd finished she fished for a handkerchief in her apron pocket.

Out fell the geranium cutting!

Mrs. Calamity picked it up and handed it to Mrs. Pepperpot. 'There—take it! I stole it from your house. Now you'd better have it back, for I shall never need geraniums or anything else in this world, I don't suppose!'

'Don't be silly,' said Mrs. Pepperpot. 'Let's forget about all this nonsense, shall we? I'm going to *give* you the cutting as a present. You plant it, and I'm sure you'll find that it'll grow into the finest flower you ever had.'

She was right. The tiny cutting grew into a huge geranium with bright red blooms, and that in spite of the fact that Mrs. Calamity not only thanked Mrs. Pepperpot, but shook hands as well, which is the worst thing you can do if you believe in bad omens.

But from then on she changed her ideas, and people no longer called her Mrs. Calamity, but plain Mrs. Brown instead.

Mrs. Pepperpot and the moose

IT WAS winter-time, and Mrs. Pepperpot was having trouble getting water. The tap in her kitchen ran slower and slower, until one day it just dripped and then stopped altogether. The well was empty.

'Ah, well,' thought Mrs. Pepperpot, 'it won't be the first time I've had this kind of trouble, and it won't be the last. But with two strong arms and a good sound bucket, not to mention the lucky chance that there's another well down by the forest fence, we'll soon fix that.'

So she put on her husband's old winter coat and a pair of thick gloves and fetched a pick-axe from the wood-shed. Then she trudged through the snow down the hill, to where there was a dip by the forest fence. She swept the snow away and started breaking a hole in the ice with the pick-axe. Chips of ice flew everywhere as Mrs. Pepperpot hacked away, not looking to left or right. She made such a noise that she never heard the sound of breaking twigs, nor the snorting that was coming from the other side of the fence.

But there he was; a huge moose with great big antlers, not moving at all, but staring angrily at Mrs. Pepperpot. Suddenly he gave a very loud snort and leaped over the fence, butting Mrs. Pepperpot from behind, so that she went head-first into a pile of snow!

'What the dickens!' cried Mrs. Pepperpot as she scrambled to her feet. But by that time the moose was back on the other side of the fence. When she saw what

it was that had pushed her over, Mrs. Pepperpot lost no time in scrambling up the hill and into her house, locking the door behind her. Then she peeped out of the kitchen window to see if the moose was still there. He was.

'You wait, you great big brute!' said Mrs. Pepperpot. 'I'll give you a fright you won't forget!'

She put on a black rain-cape and a battered old hat, and in her hand she carried a big stick. Then she crept out of the door and hid round the corner of the house.

The moose was quietly nibbling the bark off the trees and seemed to be taking no notice of her.

Suddenly she stormed down the hill, shouting, 'Woollah, Woollah, Woollah!' like a Red Indian, the black rain-cape flapping round her and the stick waving in the air. The moose *should* have been frightened, but he just took one look at the whirling thing coming towards him, leaped the fence and headed straight for it!

Poor Mrs. Pepperpot! All she could do was to rush back indoors again as fast as she knew how.

'Now what shall I do?' she wondered. 'I must have water to cook my potatoes and do my washing-up, and a little cup of coffee wouldn't come amiss after all this excitement. Perhaps if I were to put on my old man's trousers and take his gun out . . . I could pretend to aim it; that might scare him off.'

So she put on the trousers and took out the gun; but this was the silliest idea she had had yet, because, before she was half-way down the hill, that moose came pounding towards her on his great long legs. She never had time to point the gun. Worse still, she dropped it in her efforts to keep the trousers up and run back to the house at the same time. When the moose saw her disappear indoors, he turned and stalked down the hill again, but this time he didn't jump back over the fence, but stayed by the well, as if he were guarding it.

'Ah well,' said Mrs. Pepperpot, 'I suppose I shall have to fill the bucket with snow and melt it to get the water I need. That moose is clearly not afraid of anything.'

So she took her bucket and went outside. But just as she was bending down to scoop up the snow, she turned small! But this time the magic worked quicker than usual, and somehow she managed to tumble into the bucket which was lying on its side. The bucket started to roll down the hill; faster and faster it went, and poor Mrs. Pepperpot was seeing stars as she bumped round and round inside.

Just above the dip near the well a little mound jutted out, and here the bucket made a leap into space. 'This is the end of me!' thought Mrs. Pepperpot. She waited for the bump, but it didn't come! Instead the bucket seemed to be floating through the air, over the

fence and right into the forest. If she had had time to
think, Mrs. Pepperpot would have known that the
moose had somehow caught the bucket on one of his
antlers, but it is not so easy to think when you're swing-
ing between heaven and earth.

At last the bucket got stuck on a branch and the
moose thundered on through the undergrowth. Mrs.
Pepperpot lay there panting, trying to get her breath
back. She had no idea where she was. But then she heard:
'Chuck, chuck! Chuck, chuck!'—the chattering of a
squirrel as he ran down the tree-trunk over her head.

'Hullo!' said the squirrel, 'if it isn't Mrs. Pepperpot!
Out for a walk, or something?'

'Not exactly a *walk*,' said Mrs. Pepperpot, 'but I've had a free ride, though I don't know who gave it to me.'

'That was the King of the Moose,' said the squirrel. 'I saw him gallop past with a wild look in his eyes. It's the first time I have ever seen him afraid, I can tell you that. He is so stupid and so stuck-up you wouldn't believe it. All he thinks of is fighting; he goes for anything and anybody—the bigger the better. But you seem to have given him the fright of his life.'

'I'm glad I managed it in the end,' said Mrs. Pepperpot, 'and now I'd be gladder still if I knew how to get myself home.'

But she needn't have worried, because at that moment she felt herself grow large again, and the next thing she knew she had broken the branch and was lying on the ground. She picked herself and her bucket up and started walking home. But when she got to the fence she took a turn down to the well to fill the bucket.

When she stood up she looked back towards the forest, and there, sure enough, stood the moose, blinking at her. But Mrs. Pepperpot was no longer afraid of him. All she had to do was to rattle that bucket a little, and the big creature shook his head and disappeared silently into the forest.

From that day on Mrs. Pepperpot had no trouble fetching water from the well by the forest fence.

Mrs. Pepperpot finds a hidden treasure

IT WAS a fine sunny day in January, and Mrs. Pepperpot was peeling potatoes at the kitchen sink.

'Miaow!' said the cat; she was lying in front of the stove.

'Miaow yourself!' answered Mrs. Pepperpot.

'Miaow!' said the cat again.

Mrs. Pepperpot suddenly remembered an old, old rhyme she learned when she was a child. It went like this:

> The cat sat by the fire,
> Her aches and pains were dire,
> Such throbbing in my head,
> She cried; I'll soon be dead!

'Poor Pussy! Are your aches and pains so bad? Does your head throb?' she said, and smiled down at the cat.

But the cat only looked at her.

Mrs. Pepperpot stopped peeling potatoes, wiped her hands and knelt down beside the cat. 'There's something you want to tell me, isn't there, Pussy? It's too bad I can't understand you except when I'm little, but it's not my fault.' She stroked the cat, but Pussy didn't purr, just went on looking at her.

'Well, I can't spend all day being sorry for you, my girl, I've got a husband to feed,' said Mrs. Pepperpot, and went back to the potatoes in the sink. When they were ready she put them in a saucepan of cold water on the stove, not forgetting a good pinch of salt. After that she laid the table, for her husband had to have his dinner sharp at one o'clock and it was now half past twelve.

Pussy was at the door now. 'Miaow!' she said, scratching at it.

'You want to get out, do you?' said Mrs. Pepperpot, and opened the door. She followed the cat out, because she had noticed that her broom had fallen over in the snow. The door closed behind her.

And at that moment she shrank to her pepperpot size!

'About time too!' said the cat. 'I've been waiting for days for this to happen. Now don't let's waste any more time; jump on my back! We're setting off at once.'

Mrs. Pepperpot didn't stop to ask where they were going; she climbed on Pussy's back. 'Hold on tight!' said Pussy, and bounded off down the little bank at the back of the house past Mrs. Pepperpot's rubbish-heap.

'We're coming to the first hindrance,' said Pussy; 'just sit tight and don't say a word!' All Mrs. Pepperpot could see was a single birch-tree with a couple of magpies on it. True, the birds seemed as big as eagles to her now and the tree was like a mountain. But when the magpies started screeching she knew what the cat meant.

'There's the cat! There's the cat!' they screamed. 'Let's nip her tail! Let's pull her whiskers!' And they swooped down, skimming so close over Mrs. Pepperpot's head she was nearly blown off the cat's back. But the cat took no notice at all, just kept steadily on down the hill, and the magpies soon tired of the game.

'That's that!' said the cat. 'The next thing we have to watch out for is being hit by snowballs. We have to cross the boys' playground now, so if any of them start aiming at you, duck behind my ears and hang on!'

Mrs. Pepperpot looked at the boys; she knew them all, she had often given them sweets and biscuits. '*They* can't be dangerous,' she said to herself.

But then she heard one of them say: 'There comes that stupid cat; let's see who can hit it first! Come on,

boys!' And they all started pelting snowballs as hard as they could.

Suddenly remembering how small she was, Mrs. Pepperpot did as the cat had told her and crouched down behind Pussy's ears until they were safely out of range.

The cat ran on till they got to a wire fence with a hole just big enough for her to wriggle through.

'So far, so good,' she said, 'but now comes the worst bit, because this is dog land, and we don't want to get caught. So keep your eyes skinned!'

The fence divided Mrs. Pepperpot's land from her neighbour's, but she knew the neighbour's dog quite well; he had had many a bone and scraps from her and he was always very friendly. 'We'll be all right here,' she thought.

But she was wrong. Without any warning, that dog suddenly came bearing down on them in great leaps and bounds! Mrs. Pepperpot shook like a jelly when she saw his wide-open jaws all red, with sharp, white teeth glistening in a terrifying way. She flattened herself on the cat's back and clung on for dear life, for Pussy shot like a Sputnik across the yard and straight under the neighbour's barn.

'Phew!' said the cat, 'that was a narrow squeak! Thanks very much for coming all this way with me; I'm afraid it wasn't a very comfortable journey.'

'That's all right,' said Mrs. Pepperpot, 'but perhaps you'll tell me now what we've come for?'

'It's a surprise,' said Pussy, 'but don't worry, you'll get your reward. All we have to do now is to find the hidden treasure, but that means crawling through the hay. So hang on!'

And off they went again, slowly this time, for it was difficult to make their way through the prickly stalks that seemed as big as bean-poles to Mrs. Pepperpot. The dust was terrible; it went in her eyes, her mouth, her hair, down her neck—everywhere.

'Can you see anything?' asked the cat.

'Only blackness,' answered Mrs. Pepperpot, 'and it seems to be getting blacker.'

'In that case we're probably going the right way,' said Pussy, crawling further into the hay. 'D'you see anything now?' she asked.

'Nothing at all,' said Mrs. Pepperpot, for by now her eyes were completely bunged up with hay-seed and dust.

'Try rubbing your eyes,' said the cat, 'for this is where your hidden treasure is.'

So Mrs. Pepperpot rubbed her eyes, blinked and rubbed again until at last she could open them properly. When she did, she was astonished; all round her shone the most wonderful jewels! Diamonds, sapphires, emeralds—they glittered in every hue!

'There you are! Didn't I tell you I had a hidden treasure for you?' said the cat, but she didn't give Mrs. Pepperpot time to have a closer look. 'We'll have to hurry back now, it's nearly time for your husband's dinner.'

So they crawled back through the hay and, just as they got out in the daylight, Mrs. Pepperpot grew to her ordinary size. She picked the cat up in her arms and walked across the yard with her. The dog was there, but what a different dog! He nuzzled Mrs. Pepperpot's skirt and wagged his tail in the friendliest way.

Through the gate they came to the place where the boys were playing. Everyone of them nodded to her and politely said 'Good morning'. Then they went on up the hill, and there were the magpies in the birch-tree. But not a sound came from them; they didn't even seem to notice them walking by.

When they got to the house Mrs. Pepperpot put the cat down and hurried indoors. It was almost one o'clock. She snatched the saucepan from the stove—a few potatoes had stuck to the bottom, so she threw those

out and emptied the rest into a blue serving-bowl. The saucepan she put outside the back door with cold water in it.

She had only just got everything ready when Mr. Pepperpot came in. He sniffed suspiciously. 'I can smell burnt potatoes,' he said.

'Nonsense,' said Mrs. Pepperpot, 'I dropped a bit of potato-skin on the stove, that's all. But I've aired the room since, so just you sit down and eat your dinner.'

'Aren't you having any?' asked her husband.

'Not just now,' answered Mrs. Pepperpot, 'I have to go and fetch something first. I won't be long.' And Mrs. Pepperpot went back down the hill, through the gate to her neighbour's yard, and into the barn. But this time she climbed *over* the hay till she found the spot where her hidden treasure lay.

And what d'you think it was?

Four coal-black kittens with shining eyes!

Mr. Pepperpot

Now you have heard a lot about *Mrs.* Pepperpot, but hardly anything about *Mr.* Pepperpot.

He usually comes in at the end of the stories, when Mrs. Pepperpot is back to her normal size and busy with his dinner. If the food isn't ready he always says 'Can't a man ever get his dinner at the proper time in this house?' And if it is ready, he just sits down to eat and says nothing at all. If it's cold out, he says 'Brrrrrrr!' and if it's very hot, he says 'Pheeew!' If Mrs. Pepperpot has done something he doesn't like, he says 'Hmmmmm!' in a disapproving tone of voice. But if he himself is thinking of doing something he doesn't want Mrs. Pepperpot to know about, he goes round the house whistling to himself and humming a little tune.

One evening when he came home, he went up to the attic. Now, Mrs. Pepperpot had hidden four black kittens up there, because Mr. Pepperpot didn't like kittens when they were small (some people don't, you know). So, when Mr. Pepperpot came down from the attic, he stood in the middle of the floor and said 'Hmmmm!' And a little while later he started whistling and humming his tune.

Mrs. Pepperpot said nothing, though she knew what it meant. She just took his old winter coat from its peg and started mending a tear in it.

'What are you mending that for?' asked Mr. Pepperpot.

'The weather's getting so bad, you'll need it,' said Mrs. Pepperpot.

'Who said I was going out?' asked Mr. Pepperpot.

'You can do as you like,' said his wife, 'I'm staying right where I am.'

'Well, maybe I *will* take a turn outside, all the same,' said Mr. Pepperpot.

'I thought you would,' she said.

Mr. Pepperpot went back to the attic, found a big sack and popped the four kittens inside. But when he got to the bottom of the stairs, he thought he would put on the old winter coat. So he put the sack down and went into the kitchen. There he found the coat hanging over a chair.

'I'm going out now!' he called, thinking his wife must be in the sitting-room. He got no answer, but he didn't bother to call again, as he was afraid the kittens might get out of the sack which wasn't properly tied. Quickly he slung it over his shoulder and went out.

It was a nasty night; the wind blew sleet in his face and the road was full of icy puddles.

'Ugh!' said Mr. Pepperpot, 'this weather's fit to drown in!'

'Isn't that just what you're going to do to us poor kittens?' said a tiny voice close by.

Mr. Pepperpot was startled. 'Who said that, I wonder?' he said. He put the sack down to look inside, but as soon as he opened it out jumped one of the kittens and ran off in the darkness.

'Oh dear, what shall I do?' he said, tying up the sack again as quickly as he could. 'I can't leave a kitten running about on a night like this.'

'He won't get any wetter than the rest of us by the time you've finished with us,' said the little voice again.

Mr. Pepperpot untied the sack once more to find out who was speaking. Out jumped the second kitten and disappeared in the sleet and snow. While he hurriedly tied a knot to stop the rest from getting out, he said to himself:

'What if the fox got those two little mites? That would be terrible!'

'No worse than being in *your* hands,' said the tiny voice.

This time, Mr. Pepperpot was very careful to hold his hand over the opening as he untied it. But his foot slipped on the ice and jogged the sack out of his hand, and another kitten got away.

'Three gone! That's bad!' he said.

'Not as bad as it'll be for me!' came the voice from the sack.

'I know who it is now,' said Mr. Pepperpot; 'it's my

old woman who's shrunk again. You're in that sack, aren't you? But I'll catch you! You just wait!' And with that he opened the sack again.

Out jumped the fourth kitten and ran off, lickety-split!

'You can run, I don't care!' said the old man. 'I'm going to catch that wife of mine—it's all her fault!' He got down on his knees and rummaged round in every corner of the sack. But he found nothing—it was quite empty.

Now he really was worried; he was so worried he started sobbing and crying, and in between he called 'Puss, Puss!' and searched all over the place.

A little girl came along the road. 'What have you lost?' she asked.

'Some kittens,' sniffed Mr. Pepperpot.

'I'll help you find them,' said the little girl.

Soon they were joined by a little boy, and he had a torch which made it easier to search. First the little girl found one kitten behind a tree-stump, then the boy found two kittens stuck in a snow-drift, and Mr. Pepperpot himself found the fourth one and put them all back in the sack, tying it very securely this time.

'Thank you for your help,' he said to the children and asked them to take the kittens back to his house and put them in the kitchen.

When they had gone, he started looking for his little
old woman. He searched for an hour—for two hours; he
called, he begged, he sobbed, he was quite beside himself.
But in the end he had to give up. 'I'll go home now,' he
said to himself, 'and try again tomorrow.'

But when he got home, there was Mrs. Pepperpot, as
large as life, bustling round the kitchen, frying a huge
pile of pancakes! And by the kitchen stove was a wicker
basket with the mother cat and all four kittens in it.

'When did you come home?' asked the astonished
Mr. Pepperpot.

'When did I come home? Why, I've been here all the time, of course,' she said.

'But who was it talking to me from the sack, then?'

'I've no idea,' said Mrs. Pepperpot, 'unless it was your conscience.' And she came over and gave him a great big hug and kiss.

Then Mr. Pepperpot sat down to eat the biggest pile of pancakes he had ever had and all with bilberry jam, and when he was full the kittens finished off the last four.

And after that Mr. and Mrs. Pepperpot lived happily together, and Mrs. Pepperpot gave up shrinking for a very long time indeed—that's why the next story is a made-up story about an OGRE and not about Mrs. Pepperpot at all, at all.

The ogres

IT IS time we made up a story about *ogres*. You see we have to make it up, because there aren't any ogres, really.

First we must have an ogre and he must have a name. Let's call him GAPY GOB, because he's very fond of eating and is always opening his mouth for more.

Good. Gapy Gob has two servants, a little girl and a little boy. The little girl spends all *her* time cooking porridge for her master, so we can call her KATIE COOK. The little boy spends all *his* time chopping wood to burn in the stove on which Katie cooks the porridge. So we can call him CHARLIE CHOP.

Katie Cook and Charlie Chop aren't really ogres at all; they're just ordinary children, but they have no home of their own, so Gapy Gob lets them stay with him. They are very happy there, except for one thing; on the other side of the hill lives an ogress by the name of WILY WINNIE and her servant, a very cunning cat called RIBBY RATSOUP.

Now I think we have enough ogres and people to start the story, don't you?

Wily Winnie was very set on marrying Gapy Gob, because she knew he had a large ham hanging in his larder. Not only that, but Gapy Gob had a much better house than her own and she wanted to live in it. But first she had to get rid of the ogre's two servants, Katie Cook and Charlie Chop.

Several times she had tried to persuade him to send them away, but each time the children had told Gapy Gob that Wily Winnie was just after his ham and that her cat was waiting to eat up all the herrings they had salted down.

One morning early, when Gapy Gob was sitting at the table waiting for Katie to finish stirring his porridge, and

Charlie was sharpening his axe ready for the day's work,
there was a knock at the door.

'Come in,' said Katie.

The door opened, and there stood Ribby Ratsoup,
Wily Winnie's cat.

'Good morning,' she said, trying to curtsey politely,
but it was difficult because she was wearing riding-boots
and carried a large bucket over one paw.

'Good morning,' said Katie. 'If you've brought that

bucket for salt herrings, you can spare yourself the trouble; you're not having any.'

'No, no, nothing of the kind!' said the cat. 'I just called to see if anyone here would like to go bilberry-picking with me.'

'Bilberry-picking?' said Gapy Gob. 'You going bilberry-picking? What a clever cat you are! But I don't think Katie and Charlie have time to go with you today.' The ogre was a bit put out because he had had to wait for his porridge.

'I was just asking,' said Ribby in a sugary voice. 'You see, at *our* house we get up early. I get all the work done before breakfast. So my mistress told me to go berrying today, and of course I do as I am told. Well, bye-bye for now!'

When the cat had gone, the ogre said, 'I don't really see why you shouldn't go bilberrying too; they're very nice to eat. . . .' And he licked his chops.

'Just as you like,' said Charlie. 'We don't mind going. But then you'll have to look after yourself while we're out.'

'Don't touch the matches, whatever you do!' warned Katie.

'And if anybody knocks, be sure *not* to open the door,' said Charlie.

'I won't,' said Gapy Gob.

But as soon as the children had gone, Wily Winnie came panting over the hill, her skirts flying.

'Hullo, hullo! How are you, Gapy Gob?' she shouted, and marched straight into the kitchen.

Gapy Gob backed away from her into a corner. 'I'm not supposed to open the door if anyone knocks,' he said.

'Ah, but I *didn't* knock. I came straight in!' said the ogress. 'How nice to see you again, dear Gapy Gob. My cat has gone bilberry-picking, so I was all alone!'

'The children have gone as well,' said Gapy Gob.

'How lovely!' cried Wily Winnie. 'Then you can come home with me for a while. We can sit and talk while we wait for them to bring back the berries. I wonder who will bring the most? Come along now, Gapy, let me help you on with your coat. First this arm; that's right, and now this one. There now, we're ready to go!'

So Gapy Gob went home with Wily Winnie and sat in her house all day, while Katie Cook and Charlie Chop searched the wood for all the bilberries they could find. They each had a punnet to pick in, and when they were full they tipped them into their bucket which stood under a fir-tree.

But what d'you think Ribby Ratsoup had been doing all this time? Well, she hadn't been picking bilberries, I

can tell you that much! She spent the day scampering through the forest, chasing squirrels and field mice and birds. Late in the afternoon she came across the children's bucket, filled almost to the brim with bilberries. Katie and Charlie were out of sight, picking their last punnet each.

Ribby, as I told you before, was a very cunning cat. She emptied all the berries into her own bucket and one of her boots. Then she ran home to her mistress as fast as she could go.

Back in Wily Winnie's house the ogre and ogress were getting on fine together. They had come to an agreement that if the *cat* came home with most bilberries, Gapy

Gob would send Katie and Charlie away, but if the *children* had most, Ribby Ratsoup would have to go.

Suddenly they saw something come streaking across the hill-top. It was the cat with her bucket and her boot full of bilberries.

Wily Winnie clapped her hands. 'My cat's won! My cat's won! Look what a lot she's brought!'

'Ah, you wait and see what the children bring!' said Gapy Gob. He was so fond of the children, he didn't want to lose them.

A little while later they saw Katie and Charlie come over the hill-top. But they were walking very, very slowly. And their bucket was—empty.

'What did I tell you, Gapy Gob?' shouted the ogress. 'Those children are no good. Send them away, Gapy, send them away!'

So Gapy Gob went out in the yard and said to the

children: 'Charlie and Katie, you can go. I don't want you any more; you can't even pick bilberries.' And he turned away, for he had tears in his eyes.

'I see,' said Charlie.

'Very well,' said Katie.

'Ribby is much better at picking than you are,' said Gapy Gob.

'Is that so?' said Charlie. 'Then perhaps Madam Ratsoup wouldn't mind showing us her paws?'

'My paws?' said the cat. 'Certainly you can see my paws.' And she held them up.

'Hmm!' said Charlie. 'Very strange. The cat has picked a whole bucket and a boot full, yet her paws are as clean as if she'd been licking them all day. *We*, who have no bilberries to show for it, have our arms stained blue right up to the elbows. Ribby Ratsoup is a thief; she has stolen our berries and now she can give them back to us, every single one, or it will be the worse for her!'

The cat saw the game was up and quickly handed back the berries. Then the children took Gapy Gob by the hands and they all three went home together.

But Wily Winnie was so angry, she shut the cat up in the barn without any supper.

That's the end of this story. Now it's your turn to make one up about the ogres, and we'll see which is the best.

The good luck story

ONCE upon a time there was a little old woman—no, what am I saying? She was a little girl. But this little girl worked every bit as hard as any grown-up woman. Her name was Betsy; she wore a scarf round her head like the women did, and she could weed a field of turnips with the best of them. If any of the big boys started throwing stones or lumps of earth at her, she tossed her head and gave them a piece of her mind.

She was weeding in the field one day when a ladybird settled on her hand.

'Poor little ladybird! What do you want on my thumb?' said Betsy, at the same time trying to think of a really good wish. For ever since she was tiny she had been told to make a wish when a ladybird flew from her finger.

'I wish . . . I wish I had a new skipping-rope to take to school,' she said quickly. But then she remembered that she had borrowed a skipping-rope from her friend, Anna, and lost it. If she got a new one now she would *have* to give it to Anna.

The ladybird crawled slowly out on Betsy's thumb-nail, and she was terrified it would fly away before she had had time to wish for all the things she wanted. Luckily, the ladybird changed its mind when it reached the top; it crawled down again and started up the first finger.

'Now I shall wish—I wish I could have some money,' said Betsy, but was sorry as soon as she had said it. After all, she would *get* some money when she had finished her weeding. And, anyway, the money would have to go to Britta from Hill Farm to pay for the old bicycle Betsy had bought from her in the spring.

The ladybird crawled right out on the top of Betsy's first finger. Then it stopped to consider, and slowly

turned round and climbed down again to start on the second finger.

'Now I must hurry up and wish before it flies off the top of this finger,' said Betsy, while the ladybird climbed steadily upwards.

'I wish I were a real princess,' she said, but then she thought: 'How stupid of me—how can I be a real princess if I haven't been one before? Unless, of course, a prince came along and asked me to marry him. That would look funny, wouldn't it? A prince in a turnip field!' And she laughed at herself.

The ladybird was stretching one wing now and hovering.

'Don't fly yet, little ladybird! I don't want to be a princess at all. I want something quite different. I want my mother to be rid of her rheumatics when I get home tonight.'

This was a good wish, and Betsy was pleased with it. You see, it was a great trouble to her when her mother had the rheumatics; then Betsy had to dress all her little brothers and sisters and give them their dinner. It would be nice not to have to work so hard.

But the ladybird didn't take off even from this finger. Slowly it turned round and made its way to the bottom of the finger and then on to Betsy's hand. Then it stopped; it didn't seem to want to go on at all. But Betsy gave it a gentle little push and got it on to her third finger.

Now she knew what to wish; that her father could get the job he was after that day. Because if he did, he had said he would buy her a whole sheet of pictures to stick in her scrap-book.

But the ladybird had its own ideas; it crawled more and more slowly up Betsy's third finger, and every now and then Betsy had to poke it to get it out on the nail. Then all of a sudden the ladybird rolled off and fell on to the ground.

Betsy lay down flat among the turnips and managed to coax the creature on to her little finger. It didn't move. So Betsy lifted it gingerly out on the nail. Still it didn't move, and she thought she must have hurt it. 'You poor thing! Did I squeeze you too hard? Oh, please, little ladybird, do fly now! Because I want to wish that Daddy could get the job he's after!'

And suddenly the ladybird opened its wings and flew off—straight up towards the sun.

And do you know? When Betsy got home that night her mother was feeling better than she had been for a long while. Her father had got the job and had remembered the pictures for her scrap-book, and her friend Anna had been to see her. She had found the lost skipping-rope and brought it for Betsy, because she had a new one herself. Not only that, but Britta from Hill Farm had been to say that if Betsy would mind her baby for her twice that week, she needn't pay any more for the old bicycle!

What more could you want from a lucky ladybird?

Mr. Big Toe's journey

MR. BIG TOE lived with his four brothers in a little sock, and the sock lived in a shoe which belonged to a little boy who was walking down the lane eating a very big sandwich.

Mr. Big Toe said: 'Now I've been stuck in this place so long, I think it's time I did some travelling.'

When his brothers asked him where he was going, he answered: 'Oh, I expect I shall sail across the ocean.'

'But how will you get through the wall?' they asked him—they meant the sock, of course.

'That's easy for someone as big as I am. I shall just scratch a hole.'

'Will we never see you again?' asked the one who was closest to Mr. Big Toe.

'Maybe not. But I'll ring you up and tell you how I'm getting on. Well, I'm off now, so goodbye!'

Then Mr. Big Toe started scratching a hole, and it didn't take long before he had wriggled through. The rest of the toes sat waiting for the telephone message.

Soon the little boy started running and Mr. Big Toe sent his first message:

'Hullo, hullo! I've started on my travels. It feels rather strange at first, of course, and I miss you a bit. But I expect you miss me much more. Be good. I'll ring you up again when I get on the boat.'

After a time the little boy found a puddle and began dipping his shoe in it. Mr. Big Toe got on the telephone again.

'Hullo boys, I've just got to the edge of the ocean; in a few moments I'll be sailing to the far shore. It's a dangerous journey, but don't worry, I'll manage! The waves are enormous! Still, the boat seems strong and seaworthy. It won't be long now before I meet the African Chief's Big Toe and all his little black brothers. I'll tell them I've left *my* four brothers at home. They'll be glad to hear about you, I expect. . . . Bye, bye, I must ring off now till we get to the far shore.'

The boy waded out into the middle of the puddle, but it was deeper than he thought, and while the other toes were lying inside the sock, thinking of their big brother alone on the stormy sea, they had another call from him.

'Hullo there! This is getting more and more danger-ous; the boat is out in the middle of the ocean, and it's leaking badly. If you don't hear anything more for a

bit, it's because I have to use my nail to bail the water out. It's difficult, but I'm not a bit afraid!'

'Poor Big Toe!' the brothers said to each other and huddled closer together inside the sock.

The little boy had splashed through the puddle by now. Next he found a tricycle and got on it. He rode it as fast as he could and stuck both his legs straight out in the air.

Mr. Big Toe's telephone rang again. 'Hullo boys, hullo! It's your brother Big Toe calling. I'm floating in mid-air. I'm in an aeroplane, but you needn't worry, it's quite safe. The boat sank, though I did my best to bail all the water out. I was alone, you see, that made it very difficult. However, you'll be pleased to know I'm on my way home now. See you all soon!'

The boy went indoors to change his wet socks. The five toes got a new home to live in and the boy set out again with another big sandwich in his hand.

'Fancy you coming home to us!' said all the brothers to Mr. Big Toe, and they curled themselves round him to make him feel warm and cosy.

'Yes, yes, home is all right when the sock is dry and clean,' said Mr. Big Toe. 'But I don't suppose it will be long before I take another journey.'

A concertina concert

DO YOU remember the story we made up? The one about the ogres, Gapy Gob and Wily Winnie? Gapy Gob had two servants, Katie Cook and Charlie Chop, who were not ogres at all, but just ordinary children. Wily Winnie had a cat to look after her, called Ribby Ratsoup, a very cunning cat. These two would sit at home in the evenings and talk about how they could get Gapy Gob to marry Wily Winnie. Then one day, just after New Year, the cat had an idea.

'I know how to get Gapy Gob to marry you,' she said. 'Tell him you have learned to play the concertina. Gapy likes concertina music better than anything.'

'You have some bright ideas, I must say!' said Wily Winnie scornfully. 'You know I can't play the concertina.'

'Don't worry about that,' said Ribby. 'I met a musician in the forest this morning; that's what made me think of it. Wait here till I fetch him.'

So the cat went into the forest and there, under a fir-tree, sat a very small, thin musician. He had been

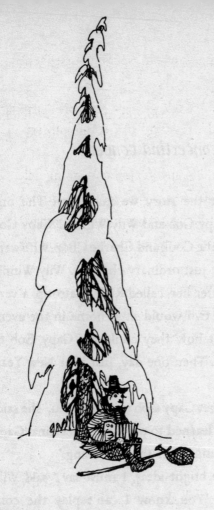

playing his concertina at village gatherings all through Christmas and now he was anxious to get home as quickly as possible. But when Ribby had met him that morning, the little musician had lost his way in the forest. So Ribby had promised to come back and guide him if he would wait there.

'You can play me a tune in return,' the cat had said.

Now, when the musician saw the cat trotting towards him he was very pleased.

'Shall I play you a tune now?' he asked.

'Not just yet,' said Ribby. 'I want you to come home with me first to eat a meal and have some coffee. Then you can play your concertina to me and my mistress.'

This sounded a good idea to the musician, who was hungry by now. But when he got to the door and saw that the cat's mistress was an ogress, he was very frightened.

At first Wily Winnie did her best to be nice to him, but as this only made him more frightened, she ordered Ribby to lock the door. 'Now,' she said to the little musician, 'you'll do as we say!' And she brought out a large orange-box and put it in the middle of the floor.

'Get in that box, quick sharp!' said the ogress. And the musician had to crawl inside, whether he liked it or not.

Then Wily Winnie said: 'You're to stay in that box and not make a sound until I give the box a kick. Then you must play "A Life on the Ocean Wave" on your concertina.'

'Do I have to sing as well?' asked the musician, whose knees were knocking together with fear.

'Certainly,' said Wily Winnie. 'What's more, you've to make up a song about Gapy Gob and me this instant

—something about how I love him and would like him to marry me.'

The musician thought as quickly as he could, and then he sang this song:

> 'Gapy Gob is bright and fair,
> Combing down his yellow hair,
> He's my ain for ever mair,
> Bonny Gapy Gob—o!'

'Not my own idea, I'm afraid,' said the musician, 'but it's rather difficult to make up songs sitting in an orange-box.'

'It'll do,' said Wily Winnie. Then she sent the cat to fetch Gapy Gob, and smartened herself up as well as she could. Suddenly she remembered she would have to have a concertina herself, or Gapy Gob would never believe she was playing it.

'I must have a concertina,' she said.

'You'll find an old broken one in my sack,' said the musician. 'It hasn't a note in it.'

'Good,' said Wily Winnie. So she sat down and waited for Ribby to come back with Gapy Gob. But they were a very long time.

'I think I shall have to go and see what has happened to my cat,' said the ogress. 'You wait there.' And she left the musician sitting in the box. He hadn't been there long, however, before the door opened. Can you guess who came in? Katie Cook and Charlie Chop.

When the cat had arrived to invite Gapy Gob to come and listen to Wily Winnie playing the concertina, the children were quite sure something was up. So they had slipped out the back way and taken a short cut through the forest to the ogress's house. They had just seen Wily Winnie leave so they knew it was safe to go in.

'I wonder what's in that orange-box?' said Charlie Chop.

'It's me!' said the musician, and he told the children the whole story of what had happened to him after he had got lost.

'I'll show you the way home,' said Katie, 'but we'll have to be quick; the others will be here any moment now. Follow me!'

The musician crawled out of the box and ran out of the house with Katie as fast as his thin legs could carry him.

Charlie had borrowed the good concertina; now he crept into the box in the musician's place.

After a time the cat came back with Wily Winnie and Gapy Gob. The ogress was in high spirits. 'Now you just listen, Gapy Gob,' she said. 'I'm going to sit on this orange-box and play "A Life on the Ocean Wave" and you'll be *amazed*.' She picked up the old broken concertina, gave the box a kick, and started pretending to play.

But what came out was *not* 'A Life on the Ocean Wave' because, of course, it was Charlie Chop who was inside the box, and he made the most horrible noise he could on the concertina.

'Oh no, please stop!' said Gapy Gob, holding his ears. 'That was the most frightful noise I ever heard!'

'Perhaps you would like me to sing for you instead,' said Wily Winnie, and gave the box another kick. This was the signal for the musician to sing his song about Gapy Gob—you know, the one that went like 'Bobby Shaftoe':

> 'Gapy Gob is bright and fair,
> Combing down his yellow hair,
> He's my ain for ever mair,
> Bonny Gapy Gob—o!'

But this is what Charlie sang instead:

> 'Gapy is the ugliest fellow,
> Ever since I first could bellow,
> I have wished he was a toad
> So I could chase him down the road.'

'Well!' said Gapy Gob. 'I must say! If you've brought me all this way to make a fool of me, I'll go home this minute, and that's flat! Toad, indeed!' And with that he stumped out of the house, slamming the door behind him.

'Wait, Gapy! Dear Gapy! I can explain!' wailed the ogress as she hurried after him. Charlie Chop took this chance to get out of the box and run home by the short cut.

All this time Ribby Ratsoup had been in the kitchen cooking a celebration feast for his mistress and Gapy Gob. She couldn't understand why everything was so quiet suddenly, so she came in to have a look. There was nobody there. Not even in the orange-box, though she got inside it to make sure.

Just at that moment Wily Winnie came back; she was *not* in high spirits *now*. 'So it's you who's been sitting in there mocking me!' she shouted. 'You wait till I get my broom! I'll give you the hiding of your life!'

Late that night, when the little musician had long since reached home, and Gapy Gob had had his supper, and Katie Cook and Charlie Chop had finished all their work for the day, two dark figures could be seen leaping from hill-top to hill-top; it was Wily Winnie chasing Ribby Ratsoup with her broom.

A birthday party in Topsy Turvy Town

IN TOPSY TURVY TOWN, where the sun rises in the West and goes down in the North, and three times fourteen is four, the Mayor was going to have his fiftieth birthday. His little girl, Trixie, was busy baking cakes, but she couldn't get on, because the Mayor *would* keep bothering her to know how much longer it would be before his birthday.

'Do stop bothering me, Daddy dear,' she said. 'When you've slept one more night it will be your birthday. So run along to your office now, please, and write out invitations to the people you want to come to your party.'

'I won't ask the Postmaster, anyway,' said the Mayor.
'Why ever not?'

'He always teases me about my big ears,' answered the
Mayor.

'That's only when he's with the Smith,' said Trixie.
'You always play perfectly well when the Smith isn't
there.'

'But I want to ask the Smith,' said the Mayor. 'I'm
sure he'll behave if he knows we're having birthday
cake.'

'Well, you'd better ask them both, then.'

'I want to ask the Doctor and the Dentist as well,' said
the Mayor.

'I only hope the Doctor will be well enough to go out,'
said Trixie. 'I spoke to his little girl yesterday, and she

told me he had had a very bad night, tossing and turning. She was afraid he might be sickening for something. But I expect you'd better ask him all the same.'

'Oh yes, otherwise he'd sulk,' said the Mayor. 'So would the Dentist.'

'You do as you like,' said Trixie, 'but you know he isn't allowed any sweet things like chocolate cake with icing on.'

'I know. But we could give him apples and rusks instead,' said the Mayor.

'That's a good idea. Are you asking any more?'

'What a question! I can't leave the Baker out, can I?'

'Now, now, that's not the way for a Mayor to talk to his little girl!' said Trixie. 'Anyway, if you ask him you can't have any more; there isn't room.' Then she told him to put the invitations through the letter-boxes and come straight home to bed to have a good sleep before the great day.

The next day the Mayor was very excited. He sat in his office and looked at the clock till it was time to go home. Then he raced back to put on his Grand Chain of Office and went and stood by the door to welcome his guests.

The first to arrive was the Smith. He had his hands in his pockets.

'Many Happy Returns of the Day,' he said.

'Thank you,' said the Mayor, holding out his hand for the present.

'Haven't brought a present,' said the Smith.

'Never mind,' said Trixie soothingly. 'Wouldn't you like to take off those big heavy boots before you come in?'

'No,' said the Smith.

'Why not?' asked the little girl.

'Hole in my sock,' said the Smith.

'You can borrow my daddy's slippers. And then what about taking your hands out of your pockets?'

'No,' said the Smith.

'Why not?'

'Dirty,' said the Smith.

'Oh, we'll soon deal with that!' said Trixie. 'You come along to the bathroom with me; I'll help you

wash them. You'll have to let the others in by yourself,
Daddy dear.'

Next came the Doctor and the Dentist. They walked
hand-in-hand and each had a little parcel under his
arm.

'Many Happy Returns,' they said, both together.

'Thank you very much,' said the Mayor, and started

unwrapping. The Doctor's present was a stethoscope,
but it was only a toy, because it was broken. The Dentist
gave him a nice thing to squirt his mouth with.

Then came the Postmaster, and he brought a packet

of stamps which were very unusual, because all the edges had been cut off.

Last of all came the Baker. He brought a large slab of chocolate, and when he had wished the Mayor many happy returns he broke the chocolate in two, gave one half to the Mayor and stuffed the other half in his pocket.

'Come in, all of you,' Trixie said, as she came out of the bathroom with the Smith. His hands were now so clean, he was ashamed to show them.

In the dining-room there was a fine spread, with a huge birthday cake in the middle of the table decorated with fifty candles.

'Now do sit down and help yourselves,' invited Trixie. 'I'm just going to telephone.' And she shut the door. She picked up the receiver. 'Hullo, can you please give me the little girl in Flat 2?'

'There you are,' said the operator.

'Hullo, is that you, Kitty? This is Trixie.'

'Oh, hullo Trixie! What do you want?'

'Could you come and help me this afternoon? My daddy is having a birthday party and there *is* so much to do!'

'Yes, all right. But I'll have to bring my doll's ironing; there's a whole heap of it,' said Kitty on the telephone.

'We can iron together, then. *I* have a whole heap to do as well,' said Trixie.

As she put the 'phone down, Trixie heard a terrible crash from the dining-room, and when she opened the door what a sight met her eyes! There was birthday cake plastered all over the walls, and cups and saucers were strewn about the floor!

'What is the meaning of this?' she demanded sternly.

It was the Postmaster who answered. 'Well, you see, the Mayor tried to blow out the candles and he couldn't do it, so we all had a go and none of us could do it. Except the Smith.'

Trixie frowned. 'How did *you* manage it when the others couldn't do it?' she asked.

'Had my bellows,' said the Smith, staring up at the ceiling.

'Oh dear,' sighed Trixie. 'I suppose I shall have to clean up the mess. But then you really must behave. I have someone coming to see me, and we shall be in the nursery. So you're not to come in there. You can play in the sitting-room when you have finished your tea.' Then she left them to get on with it.

Trixie and her friend Kitty were ironing their dolls' clothes and having a very interesting talk together when suddenly there was another awful crash from the room where the party was going on. The Mayor came and knocked on the nursery door.

'What is it?' asked Trixie.

'It's the Postmaster,' said the Mayor; 'he's started teasing me again; I want him to go home.'

Trixie had to go and make peace. 'I really don't know why you can't play nicely instead of quarrelling,' she said.

The Postmaster was standing next to the Smith, staring at the floor. The Smith was looking at the ceiling, as usual.

'What did the Postmaster say?' asked Trixie.

'He said my ears were so big he would put a stamp on my forehead and send me by air-mail,' said the Mayor.

'*We* never put stamps on people and send them by air-mail,' said the Doctor and the Dentist, both together.

'Oh, how silly!' said Trixie. 'Now please be good boys and play a game, or something. What about Blind Man's Buff? Then I'll go and cook some lovely hot sausages for you.'

Trixie called to Kitty. 'I'll have to stop ironing dolls' clothes now, I must cook the sausages.'

'I'll come and help you,' said Kitty. 'I've finished my ironing.'

'Good,' said Trixie. But no sooner had they got to work in the kitchen than the door of the sitting-room flew open, and the Baker rushed out, grabbing his coat from the peg. Then he shot through the front door and down the main stairs, taking two at a time.

'*Now* what's happened?' asked Trixie.

The Mayor, who was nearly crying, came out in the kitchen. 'The Baker snatched his present back and ran off, just because he couldn't catch any of us in Blind Man's Buff,' he said.

'Oh dear! Oh dear!' said Trixie.

'*We* don't snatch our presents back and run off home,' said the Doctor and the Dentist.

'Of course not. You're *good* boys,' said Trixie, 'and I have some nice hot sausages for you.' Suddenly she noticed the Dentist's face. 'Goodness Gracious!' she exclaimed. 'What's that swelling you have on your cheek?' She beckoned to Kitty to have a look. 'I do believe he's got an ab—ab—what's it called?'

'You mean an abscess,' said Kitty, who was very clever. She climbed on the Dentist's knee. The Dentist opened his mouth wide, and, sure enough, he had an abscess!

'You'll have to go home to your little girl at once,' said Trixie, 'and get her to pull out the tooth for you.'

'He's not the only one who'll have to go home,' said Kitty. 'Look at the Doctor, he's coming out in spots all over his face. I expect he's getting measles.'

'Goodness Gracious!' cried Trixie. 'You'll all have to go at once before you catch the measles. Hurry and get your things on!'

So they all put on their coats and shook hands and said 'thank you' before they went home.

All except the Smith. He sat in the hall and took a very long time to put on his boots.

'You must go home to *your* little girl now,' said Trixie.

'Haven't got one,' said the Smith, with his eyes on the ceiling.

Trixie and Kitty both said 'Oh, you poor thing!' and they gave him all that was left of the birthday cake and a bucket, full of sausages, to take home.

The Mayor walked round the dining-room table, scraping all the plates and drinking all the cold tea. He thought it had been a wonderful party.

Father Christmas and the carpenter

THERE was once a carpenter called Anderson. He was a good father and he had a lot of children.

One Christmas Eve, while his wife and children were decorating the Christmas tree, Anderson crept out to his wood-shed. He had a surprise for them all: he was going to dress up as Father Christmas, load a sack of presents on to his sledge and go and knock on the front door. But as he pulled the loaded sledge out of the wood-shed, he slipped and fell right across the sack of presents. This set the sledge moving, because the ground sloped from the shed down to the road, and Anderson had no time even to shout 'Way there!' before he crashed into another sledge which was coming down the road.

'I'm very sorry,' said Anderson.

'Don't mention it; I couldn't stop myself,' said the other man. Like Anderson, he was dressed in Father Christmas clothes and had a sack on his sledge.

'We seem to have had the same idea,' said Anderson. 'I see you're all dressed up like me.' He laughed and shook the other man's hand. 'My name's Anderson.'

'Glad to meet you,' said the other. 'I'm Father Christmas.'

'Ha, ha!' laughed Anderson. 'You will have your little joke, and quite right too on a Christmas Eve.'

'That's what I thought,' said the other man, 'and if you agree we can change places tonight, and that will be a better joke still; I'll take the presents along to *your* children, if you'll go and visit *mine*. But you must take off that costume.'

Anderson looked a bit puzzled. 'What am I to dress up in then?'

'You don't need to dress up at all,' said the other. 'My children see Father Christmas all the year round, but they've never seen a real carpenter. I told them last Christmas that if they were good this year I'd try and get the carpenter to come and see them while I went round with presents for the human children.'

'So he really *is* Father Christmas,' thought Anderson to himself. Out loud he said: 'All right, if you really want me to, I will. The only thing is, I haven't any presents for your children.'

'Presents?' said Father Christmas. 'Aren't you a carpenter?'

'Yes, of course.'

'Well, then, all you have to do is to take along a few pieces of wood and some nails. You have a knife, I suppose?' Anderson said he had and went to look for the things in his workshop.

'Just follow my footsteps in the snow; they'll lead you to my house in the forest,' said Father Christmas. 'Then I'll take your sack and sledge and go and knock on your door.

'Righto!' said the carpenter.

Then Father Christmas went off to knock at Anderson's door, and the carpenter trudged through the snow in Father Christmas's footsteps. They led him into the forest, past two pine-trees, a large boulder and a tree-stump. There, peeping out from behind the stump, were three little faces with red caps on.

'He's here! He's here!' shouted the Christmas children as they scampered in front of him to a fallen tree, lying with its roots in the air. When Anderson followed them round to the other side of the roots he found Mother Christmas standing there waiting for him.

'Here he is, Mum! Here's the carpenter Dad promised us! Look at him! Isn't he tall!' The children were all shouting at once.

'Now, now, children,' said Mother Christmas, 'anybody would think you'd never seen a human being before.'

'We've never seen a proper *carpenter* before!' shouted the children. 'Come on in, Mr. Carpenter!'

Pulling a branch aside, Mother Christmas led the way into the house. Anderson had to bend his long back double and crawl on his hands and knees. But once in, he found he could straighten up. The room had a mud floor, but it was very cosy, with tree-stumps for chairs, and beds made of moss with covers of plaited grass. In the smallest bed lay the Christmas baby and in the far corner sat a very old Grandfather Christmas, his red cap nodding up and down.

'Have you got a knife? Did you bring some wood and some nails?' The children wanted to know everything at once and pulled at Anderson's sleeve.

'Now, children,' said Mother Christmas, 'let the carpenter sit down before you start pestering him.'

'Has anyone come to see me?' croaked old Grandfather Christmas.

Mother Christmas shouted in his ear. 'It's Anderson, the carpenter!' She explained that Grandfather was so old he never went out any more. 'He'd be pleased if you came over and shook hands with him.'

So Anderson took the old man's hand which was as hard as a piece of bark.

'Come and sit here, Mr. Carpenter!' called the children.

The eldest one spoke first. 'D'you know what I want you to make for me? A toboggan. Can you do that—a little one, I mean?'

'I'll try,' said Anderson, and it didn't take long before he had a smart toboggan just ready to fly over the snow.

'Now it's my turn,' said the little girl who had pig-tails sticking straight out from her head. 'I want a doll's bed.'

'Have you any dolls?' asked Anderson.

'No, but I borrow the field-mice sometimes, and I can play with the baby squirrels as much as I like. They *love* being dolls. Please make me a doll's bed.'

So the carpenter made her a doll's bed. Then he asked the smaller boy what he would like. But he was very shy and could only whisper, 'Don't know.'

' 'Course he knows!' said his sister. 'He said it just before you came. Go on, tell the carpenter.'

'A top,' whispered the little boy.

'That's easy,' said the carpenter, and in no time at all he had made a top.

'And now you must make something for Mum!' said the children. Mother Christmas had been watching, but all the time she held something behind her back.

'Shush, children, don't keep bothering the carpenter,' she said.

'That's all right,' said Anderson. 'What would you like me to make?'

Mother Christmas brought out the thing she was holding; it was a wooden ladle, very worn, with a crack in it.

'Could you mend this for me, d'you think?' she asked.

'Hm, hm!' said Anderson, scratching his ear with his carpenter's pencil. 'I think I'd better make you a new one.' And he quickly cut a new ladle for Mother Christmas. Then he found a long twisted root with a crook at

one end and started stripping it with his knife. But, although the children asked him and asked him, he wouldn't tell them what it was going to be. When it was finished he held it up; it was a very distinguished-looking walking-stick.

'Here you are, Grandpa!' he shouted to the old man, and handed him the stick. Then he gathered up all the chips and made a wonderful little bird with wings outspread to hang over the baby's cot.

'How pretty!' exclaimed Mother Christmas and all the children. 'Thank the carpenter nicely now. We'll certainly never forget this Christmas Eve, will we?'

'Thank you, Mr. Carpenter, thank you very much!' shouted the children.

Grandfather Christmas himself came stumping across the room, leaning on his new stick. 'It's grand!' he said. 'It's just grand!'

There was a sound of feet stamping the snow off outside the door, and Anderson knew it was time for him to go. He said goodbye all round and wished them a Happy Christmas. Then he crawled through the narrow opening under the fallen tree. Father Christmas was waiting for him. He had the sledge and the empty sack with him.

'Thank you for your help, Anderson,' he said. 'What did the youngsters say when they saw you?'

'Oh, they seemed very pleased. Now they're just waiting for you to come home and see their new toys. How did you get on at my house? Was little Peter frightened of you?'

'Not a bit,' said Father Christmas. 'He thought I was you. "Sit on Dadda's knee," he kept saying.'

'Well, I must get back to them,' said Anderson, and said goodbye to Father Christmas.

When he got home, the first thing he said to the children was, 'Can I see the presents you got from Father Christmas?'

But the children laughed. 'Silly! You've seen them already—when you were Father Christmas; you unpacked them all for us!'

'What would you say if I told you I had been with Father Christmas's family all this time?'

But the children laughed again. 'You wouldn't say anything so silly!' they said, and they didn't believe him. So the carpenter came to me and asked me to write the story down, which I did.

Mrs Pepperpot stories by Alf Prøysen

Mrs Pepperpot, the little old lady with a BIG problem!
Any minute, she can find herself shrinking to the size of a tiny
pepperpot. And then all sorts of amazing adventures begin!

Little Old Mrs Pepperpot

How can Mrs Pepperpot visit her friends, get the supper
cooked and stop the cat from thinking she's a mouse? And
what will happen when she gets shut in the macaroni drawer?
ISBN 0 09 938050 1

Mrs Pepperpot Again

Minding the baby, catching mice and dealing with an
enormous moose are not all that easy when you're the
size of a pepperpot.
ISBN 0 09 931800 8

Mrs Pepperpot's Outing

A day out in the countryside turns into one adventure after
another for poor Mrs Pepperpot. Falling into an ice cream
mountain is no treat when you're tiny!
ISBN 0 09 957410 1

Mrs Pepperpot's Year

Mrs Pepperpot is kept busy all year round:
being adopted by a hen, saving her friend
the moose from being hunted and
cheering up a little girl in hospital.
ISBN 0 09 926727 6

"Timeless Scandinavian magic"

Stephanie Nettell
The Guardian

VAMPIRE
BOOKS
BY
Willis Hall

He's super-friendly, **SQUEAMISH** and... veggie!
Meet everyone's favourite tomato-juice-drinking
TRANSYLVANIAN: Count Alucard.
Or is that... **D-R-A-C-U-L-A?!?** *Aaaaah!!!*

Manic vampire Alucard and his buddy Henry Hollins
star in the **HORRIFYINGLY HILARIOUS** and
seriously unspooky **VAMPIRE** series, written by
Willis Hall with wacky illustrations by
Tony Ross and Babette Cole.

Bite into the **VAMPIRE** series - it's fangtastic!

THE LAST VAMPIRE   ISBN 0 09 922102 0

THE VAMPIRE'S HOLIDAY   ISBN 0 09 922112 8

THE VAMPIRE'S REVENGE   ISBN 0 09 922122 5

THE VAMPIRE'S CHRISTMAS   ISBN 0 09 922132 2

THE VAMPIRE VANISHES   ISBN 0 09 922142 X

VAMPIRE PARK   ISBN 0 09 965331 1

VAMPIRE books by Willis Hall
Out now in paperback from Red Fox, priced £3.99